Reducing Food Waste

Debbie Croft

Contents

Reducing Food Waste

Each year, around 1.3 **billion** tonnes of food is wasted throughout the world. One-third of all food that is produced is spoiled during transportation or storage, or is thrown out after it has been bought. More than half of all food that is wasted comes from households. Families can help reduce food waste by making changes to the way they plan their weekly menu, shop for ingredients and cook meals.

A lot of food that is still edible is thrown away each year.

Planning meals before heading to the shops is a good way to avoid buying more food than a family needs. A practical starting point for meal planning is to check what food items are already in the fridge and pantry. Much of the food wastage that occurs in households is due to food items not being used quickly enough, and then having to be thrown out. It is important to understand the length of time various foods can safely be stored before use.

Checking the fridge before shopping can help people avoid buying more of a food that they already have at home.

Many packaged foods have a "use-by" date. This date indicates the food is safe to eat until that date. A use-by date is most commonly seen on **perishable** foods, such as meat and dairy products. These products should only be bought if they can be eaten before their use-by date.

A use-by date on a packet of fresh pasta shows when it must be eaten by.

Dairy products like milk and yogurt are common foods that need to be eaten by their use-by date.

Some products are labelled with a "best-before" date. This means these foods will remain fresh until that date, but can also be safely eaten afterwards. However, after the best-before date, the flavours could be slightly affected, or there could be changes to the colour or texture of the product. Frozen, dried or tinned foods usually have a best-before date stamped on them.

A best-before date on a loaf of bread shows how long it will remain fresh.

When planning family meals, the items that have the nearest use-by and best-before dates should be used first to avoid wastage. Regularly checking the contents of the fridge and pantry means foods nearing their **expiry dates** can be used up first. If there is an oversupply of some food items, they could be shared with another family to reduce food waste.

Jars of sauce and tinned foods can stay fresh for much longer than other food products.

After checking which ingredients are in the pantry, a meal plan can be made for the week ahead. It is helpful to write a shopping list to take to the market or supermarket. This list should contain only the foods that are required to make the meals on the meal plan. Listing the quantities of each item also helps to reduce food waste, because then shoppers only buy what they need.

While shopping, it is a good idea to look for bags of fruit and vegetables that have slightly odd shapes and sizes. These foods are pre-packed and usually sell at a reduced price. Sometimes, they are thrown away because they look a little different from what shoppers expect, but they are still healthy and delicious. Once these foods are chopped, grated or sliced, the odd shapes or sizes are not a problem.

Oddly shaped apples still taste delicious.

People can use a shopping list on a notepad or their phone to remember the food they need to buy.

Having a well-organised shopping list can stop shoppers from buying more of items that are on special simply because these deals appear to save them money. While special deals may be tempting, if all the food isn't used and some is thrown out, a percentage of the money spent on it is wasted, as well as the food.

Energy, fertilisers and suitable land are required to produce food, and make up a large part of its total cost. However, this money is also wasted if families do not responsibly use the food they buy.

Buying lots of products that keep for a long time can be tempting, but the food sometimes isn't eaten.

After shopping, another helpful tip for reducing food waste is to put food away in the fridge and pantry in a special order. The freshest ingredients are placed at the back, and those closest to their expiry dates are placed at the front. This way, items that need to be eaten first are close at hand and more easily seen, so food is less likely to be wasted.

Also, foods need to be placed where they cannot **contaminate** other foods. For example, meat and fish products in the fridge should not be stored where they can drip onto other food items. Even the smallest drip from these products can spoil other food that would then need to be thrown out.

Salmonella is a bacteria that grows on raw or undercooked meat and can make people very sick.

It is important to store meat separately from other food.

Once meals are prepared, food might still be wasted because the **portion size** served is too large. If smaller portions are served, anyone who is still hungry can be offered a second helping. This can prevent uneaten food on someone's plate from being thrown into the bin.

Try not to accidentally serve people more food than they want to eat.

Keeping leftovers as the basis for another meal also reduces food waste. By adding other ingredients to the leftovers, a whole new dish can be created and eaten by the family. It is helpful to label the leftovers with the date they were cooked, so they can be eaten in an **appropriate** time frame and avoid being thrown out.

Finding new ways to use leftover food items that weren't needed when preparing other meals can add more variety to the food a family eats. Some websites feature recipes that allow users to search the site for specific ingredients they have on hand. Entering two or three ingredients into the search can bring up a list of suitable recipes that can be made using those ingredients.

Some websites let people check whether leftover foods can be added to a planned meal to create a new dish.

When preparing meals, there will often be some food scraps, but these can be **repurposed** rather than tossed into the rubbish bin. Small quantities of different vegetables can be combined to make a healthy soup, and vegetable peels can be made into **stock** as a base for other healthy dishes.

Common stock ingredients are onion, celery, carrot and leftover bones or meat.

Another way to repurpose food scraps is to use a compost bin. Over time, the scraps break down into compost. The compost can then be used to **nourish** the soil in a garden.

A compost bin is a great way to turn unwanted food scraps into nourishing soil for your garden.

Wasteful habits such as buying more food than a family needs, throwing away imperfect fruits and vegetables, and serving portion sizes that are too big to finish all contribute to food waste that could easily be avoided.

If all households made a **conscious** effort to reduce food waste, both the environment and people's general health would benefit.

Every year, sufficient food is produced globally to feed the entire world's population. However, many millions of people throughout the world do not get enough food to be healthy.

Large fields of yellow canola plants and wheat are used to create food for supermarkets in Australia.

Recipes for Overripe Bananas

Bananas are a **versatile** fruit. They are a healthy and delicious snack eaten raw, or they can be combined with other ingredients to make tasty sweet treats and desserts.

When bananas are left at **room temperature**, they can quickly become overripe. Their skin turns brown and the fruit inside becomes soft. Often, these pieces of fruit are thrown away because many people don't like eating overripe bananas.

To prevent this food from going to waste, overripe bananas can be used to make a loaf of banana bread or a batch of banana cookies. The banana peels can be placed in a compost bin, so there is no food waste at all.

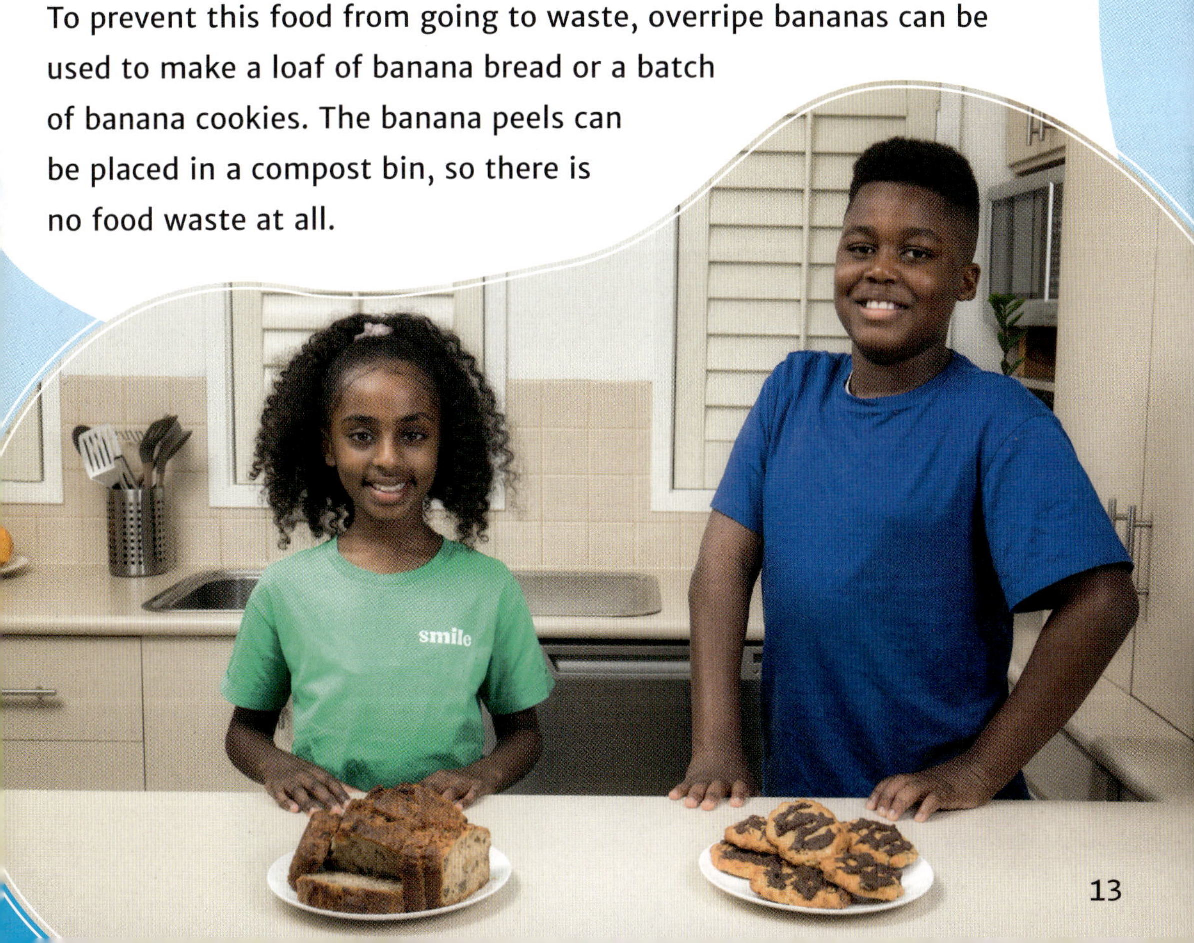

How to Make Banana Bread

Goal

To make banana bread

Equipment

- an oven
- a loaf tin
- paper towel
- a roll of baking paper, a pencil and scissors
- small, medium and large mixing bowls
- a flour sifter
- a wooden spoon
- a measuring cup
- a knife, a fork and a skewer
- a wire cooling rack

Ingredients

- 10 grams of very soft butter
- 2 cups of self-raising flour
- ¾ cup of sugar
- 1 cup of walnut pieces, **coarsely** chopped
- 2 eggs
- 3 overripe bananas
- ½ cup of vegetable oil
- 1 teaspoon of vanilla essence

Steps

1. Preheat the oven to 170 degrees Celsius.

2. While the oven is heating, grease the inside of the loaf tin by lightly spreading the butter over the base and sides, using paper towel.
3. To prevent the banana bread from burning or sticking to the tin, trace around the bottom of the tin with a pencil on a piece of baking paper. Cut out the shape and place the baking paper in the base of the tin. Cut four pieces of baking paper to cover the inner sides of the tin and extend to the top of each side. Press the paper into the buttered tin, overlapping it in the corners.

4. Sift the self-raising flour into the large mixing bowl to remove any lumps.

Sifting the flour makes the texture of the banana bread more even.

5. Add the sugar to the mixing bowl with the sifted flour and stir these ingredients with a wooden spoon until they are combined.
6. Mix the walnut pieces with the sugar and the flour.

7. Crack the eggs into a small bowl. Beat the eggs with a fork so the yolks and whites are thoroughly mixed.
8. Peel the bananas and place them in the medium-sized bowl. Mash the bananas using the fork. Add the vegetable oil, beaten eggs and the vanilla essence, and stir gently.
9. Add the banana mixture to the bowl with the flour, sugar and walnuts. Stir until all the ingredients are combined.
10. Pour the mixture into the prepared loaf tin, smoothing the top of the mixture with the back of the spoon. Ask an adult to help you place the loaf tin into the centre of the pre-heated oven to allow the mixture to cook evenly.

11. Bake the banana bread for approximately 55 minutes, or until it is golden brown on top.
12. Check that the banana bread is cooked by carefully inserting a skewer into the middle of the loaf. If the skewer comes out dry, the banana bread is cooked. If the skewer is wet, leave the banana bread in the oven for another five minutes.

Ask an adult to open the oven door and pull out the loaf tin so you can safely test the loaf with the skewer.

13. Carefully remove the hot loaf tin from the oven. Allow the banana bread to rest in the tin on the wire rack for ten minutes to cool slightly.

14. After the tin has cooled, turn the tin upside down on the rack. Slowly lift the tin off the banana bread and carefully peel the paper from the bottom and sides of the loaf. Turn the banana bread up the right way and place it on the wire rack.

15. Leave the banana bread to sit until it is cool.

16. Ask an adult to help you cut the banana bread into thick slices to serve. It can be eaten plain, with fruit yogurt or with berries. It can also be lightly toasted and buttered.

17. Store the unused banana bread in an **airtight** container at room temperature. It will last for up to four days.

18. Freeze any leftover banana bread for up to three months. When needed, remove the required number of slices from the freezer and leave them to **thaw**. This will take approximately 30 minutes.

Foods that are frozen stay fresh for much longer than if they are placed in the fridge. Meat, fruit and vegetables can all be frozen to extend their use-by dates.

How to Make Banana Cookies

Another way to use overripe bananas is to make a batch of banana cookies. These easy-to-make treats are a great addition to school lunch boxes.

Goal

To make banana cookies

Equipment

- an oven
- paper towel
- two oven trays
- a roll of baking paper and scissors
- a small and a large mixing bowl
- an electric hand mixer
- a measuring cup
- a flour sifter
- a wooden spoon, a tablespoon and a fork
- a tea towel
- a microwave oven
- a small microwave-proof bowl

Ingredients

- 10 grams of very soft butter for greasing
- 125 grams of softened butter
- $\frac{3}{4}$ cup of brown sugar
- 1 egg
- 1 cup of rolled oats
- 1 cup of self-raising flour
- 1 overripe banana
- $\frac{1}{2}$ cup of dried banana chips, roughly chopped
- 100 grams of dark chocolate buttons

Steps

1. Preheat the oven to 170 degrees Celsius.
2. Lightly grease the trays using paper towel to spread the butter.
3. Cut two pieces of baking paper the same size as the trays. Place a piece of baking paper on each tray to prevent the cookies from sticking.

Ask an adult to help with the steps involving the mixer, the hot oven and the microwave oven.

4. Put the butter and sugar into the large mixing bowl. Start the hand mixer on a slow speed to beat the butter and sugar together. Gradually increase the speed and continue beating for 2 to 3 minutes until the butter and sugar mixture is pale and **creamy**.

5. Crack the egg into the mixing bowl with the butter and sugar. Continue beating on a slow speed until the egg and the butter and sugar mixture are well combined.

6. Put the rolled oats into the mixing bowl with the butter, sugar and egg.
7. Sift the self-raising flour into the mixing bowl.

8. Use the wooden spoon to stir all the ingredients until they are well combined.

9. In the small mixing bowl, mash the banana using a fork.
10. To finish the cookie dough, carefully stir the mashed banana and the chopped banana chips into the other ingredients.

11. Cover the mixing bowl with a clean, damp tea towel. Put the cookie dough in the fridge for 45 minutes until it becomes slightly firm.

12. Remove the bowl from the fridge and divide the cookie dough into 16 portions. Roll each portion between the palms of your hands to make a ball.

13. Place the balls of cookie dough onto the prepared trays. Leave a space between each ball, so the dough has room to spread while it is cooking.

14. Use the palm of your hand to gently flatten each ball of dough until it is approximately 5 cm in diameter.

15. Bake the cookies in the oven for 12 to 14 minutes, or until they are a light golden colour. Carefully remove the trays from the oven. Leave the cookies on the trays to cool.

16. To make the topping, place the dark chocolate buttons into the small microwave-proof bowl. Put them in the microwave for ten seconds, then check and stir them. Repeat this process until the buttons are all melted.

17. Use a spoon to quickly **drizzle** the melted chocolate over the cooled cookies. Leave them to stand on the trays until the chocolate sets.

Invite your friends and family to share the banana bread and cookies. Explain that you used the overripe bananas from the fruit bowl, so they wouldn't be thrown away. Discuss some other recipes with your guests that could help reduce food waste in households.

Banana peels can also make great mulch when chopped up and placed in a layer over the soil in pot plants, but don't allow the peels to touch the plant stems! When the peels rot, they also provide nutrients for the plants.

Glossary

airtight (*adjective*) sealed to prevent air from getting in or out

appropriate (*adjective*) suitable or correct

billion (*number*) one thousand million

coarsely (*adverb*) roughly or in large pieces

conscious (*adjective*) deliberate; with awareness

contaminate (*verb*) to make dirty or unsafe

creamy (*adjective*) thick and smooth

drizzle (*verb*) to pour a small amount of liquid

expiry dates (*noun*) the dates after which foods should not be used or eaten

nourish (*verb*) to give something what it needs to grow and stay healthy

perishable (*adjective*) likely to go off quickly

portion size (*noun*) the amount of food given to one person

repurposed (*verb*) reused in a different way

room temperature (*noun*) the level of warmth in a room without heating or cooling

stock (*noun*) flavoured liquid made from meat or vegetables that is used in soup

thaw (*verb*) to change from being frozen to being liquid or soft

versatile (*adjective*) able to be used for many things

Index